Whispers
of Murder

Whispers
of Murder

PENELOPE LOVELETTER

LOVELETTER

PUBLICATIONS

EST. 2023

LOVELETTER
PUBLICATIONS

EST. 2023

Original Text by Penelope Loveletter
The moral rights of the author have been asserted.
Cover design by Penelope Loveletter

Dedicated to
bakers of cinnamon rolls
everywhere.

Chapter 1

In the heart of the charming town of Whispering Pines, Minnesota, Emma Harper started her day at Northern Pines Pastry, the beloved bakery she owned. The scent of freshly baked pastries filled the air, and the cozy atmosphere of the bakery welcomed regulars and newcomers alike.

The cheerful jingle of the bakery's doorbell announced the arrival of the morning crowd. Emma, with a flour-dusted apron and a warm smile, greeted the familiar faces.

"Morning, Emma! What's the special today?" called out Mrs. Johnson, a regular customer known for her love of cinnamon rolls.

"Today's special is my twist on a classic – cranberry orange scones. Guaranteed to brighten your day!"

As Emma plated a warm scone for Mrs. Johnson, the door swung open again. This time, it was Jim, a local handyman who always had a knack for making people laugh.

"Emma, you've got the magic touch with these pastries! They're like a spell for happiness."

Emma playfully retorted, "Well, Jim, if my pastries are magic, then you must be the wizard who sprinkles the laughter dust around here!"

The banter continued as Emma served customers, her bakery becoming a hub of lively conversation and the clinking of coffee mugs. Bridget, a young college student, chimed in, "Emma, these pastries should come with a warning – addictive and impossible to resist!"

With a grin, Emma replied, "Consider yourself warned, Bridget. I'm not responsible for any pastry addictions, though!"

Amidst the lively atmosphere, Emma's friend, Izzy, walked in. The two friends exchanged smiles, and Izzy's eyes darted toward the basement stairs. A knowing look passed between them.

"Izzy, you're just in time for the unveiling of the cranberry orange scones," Emma announced with a flourish.

Izzy grinned, "You know I can never resist your creations, Emma. They're like tiny bites of heaven."

As the morning rush continued, the aroma of coffee mingled with the sweet scent of pastries, creating a symphony of comforting smells. Emma's friend, Jake, manned the cash register, occasionally sharing a lighthearted joke with the customers.

"Jake, any new creations from Emma today?" asked Daniel Lindberg, the town's friendly detective, as he sipped his coffee.

Jake grinned mischievously, "Well, Detective Lindberg, Emma's working on a super-secret pastry that might just solve the mystery of why you can't resist coming here every morning!"

The detective laughed, "You got me there, Jake. Emma's pastries are my only weakness."

As the morning rush subsided, Emma joined Izzy at a corner table for a well-deserved break. The two friends sipped coffee, and Izzy discreetly slid a small key across the table.

Emma raised an eyebrow, "What's this?"

Izzy replied mysteriously, "Found it in the basement. Thought you might want to take a look. I went down to grab more flour, and behind one of the bags, I found this key."

Emma examined the key, a sense of intrigue settling in. "Well, this just got interesting. I'll have to take a trip to the basement later and see what this key unlocks."

Curiosity piqued, Emma slipped into the basement the first chance she got. She saw a wooden box behind the dozens of sacks of flour that were stacked so meticulously along the shelves at the back of the storage room that she had never noticed before. Emma carefully opened the box, revealing a dusty diary. Sitting on an overturned crate, Emma flipped through the pages.

As she absorbed the diary's contents, the door at the top of the stairs creaked open, and Izzy's voice echoed down, "Emma, you down there? Remember, there are customers up here too!"

Emma, snapped out of her reverie, hastily tucked the diary into her apron pocket and called back, "Coming, Izzy! Just lost track of time in this basement maze."

Ascending the stairs, she reentered the warmth of the bakery, where the doorbell jingled a cheerful welcome. Mrs. Johnson, always eager for a morning treat, greeted Emma with a smile, "Emma, those cranberry orange scones are a triumph! You've truly outdone yourself."

With a twinkle in her eye, Emma replied, "Well, Mrs. Johnson, just trying to keep the town sweet one pastry at a time."

The regular banter continued, creating a lively atmosphere. Emma moved behind the counter, deftly handling orders and engaging in friendly exchanges. As the bakery bustled around her, the diary rested inconspicuously in her apron pocket, its secrets temporarily hidden amidst the aroma of fresh-baked delights.

Bridget, the college student with an insatiable sweet tooth, teased, "Emma, any top-secret pastries in the works for the festival?"

Emma winked, "Well, if I told you, Bridget, they wouldn't be top-secret anymore, now would they?"

The day flowed in its usual rhythm, customers coming and going, sharing laughs and stories with Emma. The close-knit nature of Whispering Pines was palpable. Emma navigated through the familiar tasks, the thoughts of the hidden diary momentarily pushed to the background.

Chapter 2

That night, after the bakery was locked up, and Emma was in her upstairs apartment, she found herself engulfed in the secrets of the hidden diary. Nestled in her bed, a solitary lamp casting a soft glow, she read the words that revealed the familial strife between two prominent families in Whispering Pines, the Lindbergs and the Birches.

As the quiet hours unfolded, Emma's eyes danced over the yellowed pages, uncovering a history entrenched in conflict. The Birches, pillars of the community with their wealth and influence, clashed with the humble Lindbergs over a contested piece of land, now an integral part of the town's picturesque landscape. The diary painted a vivid picture of courtroom dramas, bitter battles, and a persistent hatred that lingered like an unhealed wound within the heart of Whispering Pines.

Emma finally drifted off to sleep in the wee hours of the morning, the old diary falling open on the bed beside her.

The next morning, although she was very tired from being up late reading, Emma meticulously mixed ingredients, the rhythmic whir of the mixer blending with the hum of her thoughts. The diary's tales lingered in her mind, casting a shadow over the festival preparations.

As Emma worked, Izzy's voice came through the screen door, "Emma, you still working? Summer Festival preparations are in full swing all over town!"

Emma wiped her hands on her apron and pushed open the door.

Izzy, with a mischievous grin, handed Emma a stack of pastry boxes, "You've got a delivery to make! Mrs. Johnson ordered a dozen of your special cranberry orange scones for the festival committee meeting."

Emma said, "Well, you know what they say, the way to a committee's heart is through their stomachs. And where is Ethan? I thought he would be with you this morning."

Izzy's boyfriend, Ethan was an artist from Minneapolis to had recently resettled in whispering Pines. "He's back in Minneapolis, taking care of some business for a few days. He called this morning to see how much he misses your cinnamon rolls!"

Emma laughed as she packaged up the cranberry orange scones for Mrs. Johnson and headed out the door.

The delivery completed, Emma hurried to return to her bustling bakery. Mrs. Johnson, ever the enthusiast, called after her, "Emma, these scones are heaven-sent! The festival committee will be singing your praises."

As Emma arranged her pastries in the window display, Detective Lindberg strolled in, drawn by the irresistible aroma. He grinned, "Emma, you're turning this town into a sugar paradise. What's your secret?"

Emma smirked, "If I told you, Detective, I'd have to make you sign a nondisclosure agreement. How can I help you today?"

"I would just like an order of cranberry scones for the office, please. And one of your cinnamon rolls for myself."

With the festival eve upon them, the town's excitement reached a crescendo. Emma, amid the swirl of pastry boxes and festival decorations, felt the excitement in the air. As she closed the bakery for the night, she felt the diary in her apron pocket. Although she hadn't finished reading it, it would have to wait. Right now she had a the Whispering Pines Summer Festival to see to.

Chapter 3

The morning sun bathed the shores of Whispering Pines Lake in a golden glow as the town gathered for the much-anticipated Summer Festival. Emma, clad in a clean new apron, stood behind the counter of Northern Pines Pastry, a delightful array of cinnamon rolls, pastries, and scones displayed before her. The festival, held right on the contested land that had been at the heart of the Lindberg-Birch feud, buzzed with excitement.

As the first customers approached, Emma couldn't help but marvel at the beauty of the lake and the tranquil setting for the festival. Mrs. Johnson, always the early bird, approached with a twinkle in her eye, "Emma, these scones you brought by are a masterpiece! How do you make them so irresistible?"

Emma grinned, "Ah, Mrs. Johnson, that's a closely guarded secret. But I'm glad you enjoy them. How many would you like today?"

Meanwhile, Jim, the local handyman, approached, eyeing the pastries with appreciation. "Emma, you're turning this festival into a haven for sweet tooths. Got anything to fix my sister's cranky spirits?"

Emma chuckled, "I promise these cinnamon rolls are a cure for the soul. How about a cinnamon roll to lift your spirits?"

As the day unfolded, Emma's bakery became a hub of laughter and camaraderie. Bridget approached, wide-eyed,

"Emma, this festival is like a dessert paradise! Which one is your personal favorite?"

Emma pointed to the cinnamon rolls, "Those are my weakness. Can't resist the gooey goodness. But go ahead, take your pick, and let me know your favorite!"

Amidst the festivities, a familiar face approached the counter. Nathan Birch, a town local known for being a local peacemaker, greeted Emma with a warm smile, "Hey, Emma! Heard you're the go-to for the best cinnamon rolls in town. Mind if I grab a couple?"

Emma beamed, "Nathan! Absolutely, help yourself. It's the festival, and everyone deserves a treat."

As Nathan enjoyed his cinnamon rolls, Emma couldn't help but notice the sense of unity that the festival brought. And Nathan was the perfect example. He was a Birch, but he went out of his way, especially recently, to be friendly with the Lindbergs.

As Emma took a leisurely break from her bustling pastry booth, she wandered through the lively fairgrounds, eager to explore the diverse offerings of her fellow vendors. The vibrant tapestry of sights, sounds, and enticing aromas greeted her at every turn.

First, she stumbled upon Isaac's fresh produce stand, where an array of colorful fruits and vegetables beckoned festival-goers. Emma marveled at the plump, sun-kissed tomatoes and the crisp greens that seemed to burst with vitality. Isaac, a weathered farmer with dirt-stained hands and a hearty laugh, shared tales of cultivating the very crops that now adorned his stand. Emma couldn't resist picking up a few ripe peaches, savoring their juicy sweetness.

Next, she found herself drawn to Maria's vibrant floral booth, a riot of colors beneath a cheerful striped canopy. Buckets of freshly cut blooms exuded the fragrance of spring, and Emma couldn't help but smile as she admired the artistry of Maria's floral arrangements. Maria, with her hands adorned in soil and petals, shared the stories behind each bloom, infusing the air with the scent of nature's beauty.

A little farther along, Emma encountered Sam's woodworking haven. The earthy aroma of freshly cut wood enveloped her as she admired the intricately carved creations on display. Sam, a craftsman with calloused hands and a keen eye for detail, spoke passionately about his love for transforming raw timber into functional art. Emma left with a hand-carved wooden spoon, a unique piece to adorn her kitchen.

Approaching Lucille Birch's booth, she was captivated by the display of delicious homemade bread. The loaves, adorned with a golden crust and emitting an irresistible fragrance, were a testament to Lucille's culinary prowess. Signs proudly declared the bread's heritage, a nod to Lucille's longstanding presence in the Whispering Pines community.

"Hello, Lucille! Your bread looks absolutely divine. How do you manage to make it so irresistible?" Emma inquired, her eyes lighting up with genuine curiosity.

Lucille, with her silver hair and a warm smile, responded, "Oh dear, it's all about the secret family recipes. Passed down through generations, you know. I can't share my secrets with the competition."

Emma left, but as she talked with Lucille, the old woman's hands, once sure and steady, now displayed a slight tremor.

"These recipes must hold so much history. Do you have a personal favorite among them?" Emma asked, noticing the fleeting glimmer of hesitation in Lucille's eyes.

Lucille, despite the momentary lapse, responded with enthusiasm, "Oh, my dear, they're all my favorites! But the herb-infused one, it's a family treasure."

As Emma left the booth with a loaf of Lucille's signature bread, she hurried back to see how her own booth was doing.

When she got back, Jim came to see her. "Lucille isn't what she used to be." he said. "She's getting dementia. Kind of sad."

"Was that the look in her eye?" Emma asked. "I wondered. She looked a little confused sometimes."

"Yes," Jim said, "she's definitely getting older. As we all are!" He laughed. "But not all of us are getting dementia like Lucille."

Suddenly, the lively ambiance was shattered by a piercing scream that echoed through the festival grounds. The festive atmosphere turned to hushed murmurs and uneasy glances as festival-goers turned their attention towards the source of the disturbance.

Emma's heart raced as she abandoned her booth, weaving through the crowd to reach the commotion. As she approached, she saw a group of onlookers gathered near the lake's edge, their faces etched with shock and horror.

"What happened?" Emma asked, her voice trembling with a mix of concern and fear.

A tearful bystander pointed towards the shoreline, "It's Nathan! He's... he's..."

Emma's eyes widened in disbelief as she followed the pointed finger. There, on the tranquil shores of the lake, lay Nathan Birch's lifeless body, a stark contrast to the lively festivities surrounding them.

The news of Nathan's murder spread like wildfire through the festival, igniting a wave of shock and disbelief. Whispers and gasps rippled through the crowd as they grappled with the grim reality that a man known for promoting peace and unity had met such a violent end.

Families gathered their children close, and concerned murmurs filled the air.

"Can you believe this? Nathan, of all people!" Mrs. Johnson exclaimed, her hands covering her mouth in horror.

Jim shook his head, "I can't wrap my head around it. Poor Nathan."

Emma overheard snippets of conversation as she tried to make sense of the unfolding tragedy.

"I just spoke to him this morning..."

"He was planning to contribute to the festival..."

"This can't be real..."

Detective Lindberg arrived at the scene, his brow furrowed with determination. He approached Emma, his expression grave.

"Did you see anything unusual before the scream?" he inquired, his gaze searching for any clues.

"No, Detective. Everything was normal. It happened so fast," Emma replied, her eyes fixed on the crime scene.

As the news spread, the festival transformed from a celebration of sweetness to a somber gathering of a grieving community. The booths, once bustling with joy, now stood in eerie silence as the reality of Nathan's murder cast a heavy shadow over Whispering Pines.

Bridget approached Emma, her eyes wide with disbelief. "How could this have happened?"

Emma shook her head, "I don't know, Bridget. But this is a tragedy, and we need to find out who did this to Nathan."

Detective Lindberg and his colleagues began securing the crime scene. The townsfolk, still processing the shocking turn of events, spoken hashed voices as they cleaned up the festival.

As the sun dipped below the horizon, casting long shadows over the lake, Whispering Pines community members put away the booths and Emma packed up the pastries and other vendors boxed up all of the homemade items and went back to their houses to ponder what had happened to Nathan.

Emma, with a heavy heart, returned to her bakery after the somber events at the festival. The usual joyous chatter of customers had been replaced by an air of melancholy, and she couldn't shake the weight of the tragedy that had befallen Whispering Pines.

Unpacking her booth items, she carefully arranged the remnants of the festival – a few unsold pastries, a display of her famous cinnamon rolls, and a lingering scent of sweetness.

The soft jingle of the bakery's bell announced the arrival of Izzy, Jake, and Bridget. Emma looked up from the counter, her eyes meeting theirs, and a silent understanding passed between friends.

Izzy was the first to reach Emma, wrapping her in a comforting hug. "What a horrible day," she whispered, her voice filled with sincerity. "I just got off the phone with Ethan. I told him what happened. He's as shocked as we are."

Jake and Bridget came in as well. The trio then gathered around the inviting kitchen table. As they settled into their seats, Emma felt a sense of gratitude for the bonds that held them together. The familiar surroundings provided a haven for collective strength.

"I still can't believe it," Izzy said, her voice filled with a mixture of sorrow and disbelief. "Nathan had been trying to make peace between the Lindbergs and the Birches. Why would someone want to hurt him?"

Bridget nodded in agreement, "Yeah, he was actively working on reconciliation. It's strange. What could have triggered this violence?"

Emma placed the tray of cinnamon rolls in the center of the table, a small attempt to bring a sense of normalcy to their gathering. "I overheard someone say that his body was found on the contested land, the very source of the feud between the Lindbergs and the Birches."

Jake furrowed his brow, "That's too much of a coincidence. The feud and Nathan's murder happening on the same land? There has to be a connection."

As they each took a cinnamon roll, Emma couldn't shake the weight of the situation. "I didn't know Nathan was trying to mend the feud. Was this a recent development? I know he had been reaching out to the Lindbergs. I wonder if he uncovered something in the process, something that led to his murder."

Izzy said, "Maybe Nathan left something behind that could shed light on why he was trying to bring them together."

As they continued their discussion, sharing memories of Nathan and speculating on the motives behind his murder, the warmth of friendship and the comforting aroma of cinnamon rolls created a sense of solace in the midst of uncertainty.

Jake, breaking the somber mood with a touch of humor, said, "You know, if Nathan were here, he'd probably be telling us not to dwell on the sadness but to focus on bringing people together."

Izzy smiled, "He always had a way of seeing the silver lining. Let's honor him by finding out the truth and bringing peace to Whispering Pines."

The group raised their cups in a silent toast to Nathan and their shared determination to uncover the mysteries surrounding his murder.

Chapter 4

The next day, the familiar hum of the bakery's activity had dimmed as the day drew to a close. Emma wiped down the countertops as Izzy, Bridget, and Jake gathered around the kitchen table. Bridget had brought a delicious smelling casserole with her. As the friends thanked Bridget for bringing such a tasty dinner, the heavy topic of Nathan's murder lingered in the air, casting a somber veil over the usually lively atmosphere.

"I can't stop thinking about it," Izzy admitted, her gaze fixed on the plate before her.

Bridget nodded, "It's like a dark cloud over Whispering Pines. We need to do something."

Emma had a sudden realization. "There might be something in the diary that can help us understand what happened. I'll go get it."

She hurried upstairs to her living quarters, retrieving the weathered diary from a small box. Returning to the kitchen, she placed it on the table, the worn leather cover hinting at the secrets held within its pages.

"What's this?" Jake asked, intrigued.

"It's a diary I found in the basement. I think it belonged to the previous owner of the bakery. It might have some clues about the feud and what happened to Nathan," Emma explained, opening the diary to its first page.

As they delved into the entries, the words from a different era came to life. The author, writing many years ago, expressed frustration and sorrow about the longstanding feud between the Lindbergs and the Birches. Cryptic passages hinted at a tragic event, a secret that could never be shared, but the details remained elusive.

"This person seems deeply affected by the feud. But what happened?" Bridget wondered aloud.

Jake, who had been silently flipping through the pages of the diary, interjected, "There's no clear indication of who owned the diary, but it's written during a time when the Lindberg-Birch feud was at its peak. There's mention of a significant incident, but no specifics. It seems like they may have been a previous owner of this very bakery. That would explain why the diary was here."

Emma's eyes narrowed as she absorbed the words, "I bought the bakery from Mr. Johnson. But I don't know who owned it before him. He mentioned that he had only owned it for a couple of years. Could there be a connection between what happened then and Nathan's murder now?"

"That's possible," Izzy said. "But it seems a little unlikely. This diary seems to have been written a very long time ago. I can't imagine that it has anything to do with Nathan's murder just yesterday."

Jake looked up with a glimmer of determination, "I might be able to access some of Nathan's computer records. He brought his laptop in for some repairs, and it's still in my shop. I can see if there's something in there that can help us connect the dots."

The soft chime of the bakery's bell announced the entrance of Detective Lindberg. Emma looked up and greeted him with a warm smile.

"Detective Lindberg! What brings you by?" she asked.

"Just in need of some comfort food, Emma. Your cinnamon rolls have a way of making a tough day a bit better," he replied, a faint smile playing on his lips.

As Emma packaged the cinnamon rolls, Detective Lindberg joined the gathering at the kitchen table. Izzy, Bridget, and Jake offered friendly nods, acknowledging his presence.

"Nathan's murder. It's a tragedy," Detective Lindberg said. "Everyone in town has an opinion, but no one seems to have any actual information."

"We're trying to make sense of it ourselves," Bridget admitted, motioning for him to take a seat. "Emma found an old diary in the bakery's basement. It seems to be from the time of the Lindberg-Birch feud."

Detective Lindberg's eyebrows raised in mild surprise, "An old diary, huh? That's quite a find. What does it say?"

Emma explained, "The entries are from years ago, during the peak of the feud. The author is upset about something that happened, but the details are unclear."

The detective leaned back in his chair, contemplating the information. "It's interesting, but I doubt it has anything to do with Nathan's murder. That's a long time ago, and we're dealing with a different set of circumstances now."

Izzy nodded in agreement, "I thought the same thing, Detective. It's just that the coincidence of finding this diary and then Nathan being murdered on the contested land—it's hard to ignore."

Detective Lindberg's gaze shifted from the diary to Emma, "If you do find anything relevant, please let me know. I can't officially comment on an ongoing investigation, but I'd appreciate any leads you might uncover."

As he picked up the box of cinnamon rolls, the conversation shifted to lighter topics. They discussed the upcoming canoe trip to the Boundary Waters, and the art show by Izzy's boyfriend, Ethan, that had just helped save the town's library.

"I'll take a few of these cinnamon rolls to go. They're too good to resist," he said, a genuine smile breaking through the professional demeanor.

Emma handed him the box, "On the house, Detective. Enjoy, and if you ever need more, you know where to find us."

With a nod of thanks, Detective Lindberg bid them farewell, the bakery's bell chiming softly as he stepped outside. As the door closed, the friends agreed that it was probably time to call it a night. They said goodbye and Emma gathered up her things, cleaned up the kitchen, and headed off to bed.

Chapter 5

Two days later, the rhythmic hum of the bakery's activities filled the air, the comforting scent of pastries wafting through the cozy space. It seemed the whole town was in need of comfort, food, much like Detective Lindberg. So, Northern Pines Pastries was even more busy than usual. The day carried on in its usual bustling manner, with customers coming and going, their laughter and whisper to gossip about the murder mingling with the occasional clatter of trays and the soft melody playing in the background.

Emma, immersed in her daily routine, was behind the counter, deftly serving customers with a warm smile. The atmosphere was one of comfort, routine, and the familiar charm of Northern Pines Pastries.

Suddenly, the bakery door swung open, and Bridget rushed in with an urgency that disrupted the otherwise tranquil scene. Her face was flushed, eyes wide with disbelief, as she approached Emma.

"Emma, you won't believe what I just heard on campus," Bridget exclaimed, her voice hushed with a mix of shock and concern.

Emma, intrigued and a bit taken aback by Bridget's urgency, gestured for her to step into the back of the bakery, away from the prying ears of the customers. As they entered the quieter space, Bridget leaned in, her expression serious.

"I overheard some people from the police department talking. They said Nathan's autopsy results came back, and it's not good. Traces of a lethal substance were found in his system. It looks like rat poison. He might have been poisoned during the festival!" Bridget's eyes searched Emma's. "How could that be? Who would ever think of poisoning Nathan?"

Emma's heart skipped a beat as the weight of Bridget's words settled in. Poisoned? The revelation sent shockwaves through her, and she instinctively glanced around to ensure no one else overheard.

"Are you sure, Bridget? Poisoned?" Emma asked, her voice a hushed whisper.

Bridget nodded solemnly, "I wish I wasn't. It's all over campus, and they're saying it was during the festival. This is bad, Emma. Really bad."

A mixture of emotions swept over Emma – disbelief, concern, and a growing sense of unease. The Summer Festival, the very event that usually brought joy and unity, now carried the sinister possibility of being the stage for a heinous crime.

"We need to find out more. If Nathan was poisoned, there's something seriously wrong here." Emma declared. "How can we know if he was the intended target? What if he ate something poisoned that was intended for someone else? Or that wasn't supposed to be eating at all!"

Bridget nodded in agreement, "This is really scary. We definitely need to figure out what's going on."

The two friends returned to the front of the bakery, their expressions now clouded with determination. The warmth of the familiar surroundings juxtaposed with the chilling revelation that lingered in the air.

The familiar jingle of the bakery's bell announced the arrival of Detective Lindberg. Emma, already on edge after Bridget's shocking revelation, wasn't entirely surprised to see him. However, the gravity of the situation escalated when Officer Blankenship followed closely behind, his stern expression casting an ominous shadow over the usually warm atmosphere.

Emma approached them, a sense of foreboding settling in her stomach. "Detective Lindberg, Officer Blankenship, what brings you here?"

Detective Lindberg avoided her eyes, a subtle tension in his posture. Officer Blankenship, on the other hand, looked stern and accusatory. "Emma Harper, you need to shut down the bakery. We're declaring it a potential crime scene," he declared, his voice authoritative.

Emma's eyes widened in shock, "What? Why?" Then in a quieter voice, she asked, "What's going on?"

"We received information that Nathan Birch bought a pastry from your bakery on the day he died. Now, we need to investigate if there's any connection between what he consumed and the poison found in his system," Officer Blankenship explained, his tone leaving little room for argument.

Emma's heart raced, her mind struggling to process the sudden turn of events. "But that doesn't make sense. Why would my pastries be involved? This is a mistake!"

"We can't discuss details here," Detective Lindberg interjected, finally meeting her gaze with a pained expression. "We need to clear the bakery and conduct a thorough investigation."

Emma, flustered and upset, turned to her customers, who had started to sense the tension in the air. "I'm sorry, everyone. We need to close for the day. Please, come back tomorrow."

"I don't think your store is going to be open tomorrow, Emma," Detective Lindberg said with a sad smile. "We can talk more about it in a few minutes."

The customers, confused and curious, filed out of the bakery, leaving Emma alone with Detective Lindberg and Officer Blankenship. The air in the bakery grew heavier with each passing moment.

Once the last customer had left, Emma turned to the law enforcement officials, her frustration evident. "Now, will someone please tell me what's going on?"

Officer Blankenship, his tone accusatory, spoke up, "People saw Nathan buying a pastry from here on the day he died. We need to investigate every possibility. We can't rule anything out."

Emma's eyes widened in disbelief, "But that doesn't mean my bakery is involved in his death. This is my livelihood, and you're shutting it down without any evidence!"

Detective Lindberg, his voice a low murmur, tried to offer some reassurance, "Emma, we have to follow protocol. Let us do our job, and we'll get to the bottom of this."

Emma, feeling cornered and frustrated, clenched her fists. "I want to be a part of this investigation. I want to know what's happening in my own bakery."

Officer Blankenship, stern-faced, replied, "I'm sorry, but you can't be involved. It's a conflict of interest. We'll update you when we have more information."

As the investigators began their work, sealing off sections of the bakery and collecting samples for analysis, Emma stood there, her frustration mounting. The once warm and inviting space now felt cold and unwelcoming. "I live upstairs, you know! You can't just kick me out. What am I supposed to do?"

Detective Lindberg, avoiding her gaze, muttered, "I'll keep you informed, Emma. Just give us some time. In the meantime, you can come and go through your private entrance. But we do need you to stay out of the bakery."

With that, Emma watched as her bakery was transformed into a crime scene.

Chapter 6

As the police meticulously investigated her bakery and the festival area, Emma, Izzy, and Jake found themselves ensnared in the web of suspicion. The poisoned item's potential origin from Emma's bakery subjected her and her friends to intense scrutiny. Although it was summer, the once warm and welcoming streets of Whispering Pines now felt frigid as Emma ventured out, the weight of accusing gazes and hushed whispers clinging to her every step.

Emma walked through the town, the usual camaraderie replaced by an uncomfortable silence that spoke louder than words. People glanced away, their conversations hushed as she passed. The suspicion hung in the air, and Emma could almost taste the bitterness of judgment on the wind.

At the local coffee shop, Izzy and Jake awaited her arrival. The familiar bell chimed as Emma entered, and her friends looked up, expressions mirroring the shared sense of isolation. They exchanged knowing glances, silently acknowledging the unspoken ostracism they faced.

"Where is Bridget" Emma asked.

"I think she's studying," Izzy said. "Maybe she's keeping her head down with all the suspicion going around."

"So," Jake began, his voice low, "you've noticed? It's like people have put up invisible walls. No one wants to talk to us."

Izzy sighed, a mixture of frustration and determination in her eyes. "How could we not notice? It's like they think we're the ones who poisoned Nathan. But we didn't, and we need to prove that."

The trio huddled around a small table, the atmosphere heavy with both the aroma of coffee and the weight of their predicament.

Emma added, "We can't let this stop us. We need to find out who did this to Nathan and clear our names. We owe it to him and to ourselves."

As the sun dipped below the horizon, casting a warm glow over Whispering Pines – that was, unfortunately, not mirrored in the faces of the people she passed—Emma made her way home.

As she was about to get ready for bed, a soft knock on her door echoed through the small entryway, and Emma couldn't help but feel a twinge of nervousness as she opened it.

Detective Lindberg stood in the doorway, looking nervous. "Can we talk privately?" he inquired.

Emma ushered him inside, and they moved to the living room, where Detective Lindberg cleared his throat before speaking.

"I want you to know, Emma, that this investigation doesn't mean I think you're guilty. It's just a necessary part of the process," he assured her.

Emma nodded, appreciating the assurance. However, she couldn't ignore the subtle shift in the detective's demeanor. His gaze lingered a little longer than strictly professional, and Emma felt a flush creeping up her cheeks.

"I understand. I just want to help find the real culprit. I know I didn't have anything to do with Nathan's death," she stated.

As the conversation unfolded, Detective Lindberg said he couldn't share the details of the investigation, but he assured her that he was looking into every other possibility, since he felt certain she could not be the murderer.

Emma couldn't help but notice the detective standing a little closer than necessary. His eyes, which she had never truly noticed before, seemed to carry a depth of sincerity. Emma found herself feeling a little self-conscious around him and wondering why.

"I appreciate your cooperation, Emma. I'll do my best to wrap this up as soon as possible," he said.

As he made his way toward the door, there was a lingering hesitation. Emma caught a glimpse of something in his eyes—perhaps a hint of sadness or understanding. She wondered if he, too, felt the peculiar atmosphere that had settled in her living room.

"Thank you, Detective. If you need anything from me, I'm here," she offered.

With a nod, Detective Lindberg bid his farewell, leaving Emma alone with a mix of conflicting emotions. The evening air seemed charged as she closed the door behind him.

The next day, the familiar bell chimed as Jake entered the coffee shop, joining Emma, Izzy, and Bridget at their usual corner table. Tensions lingered, but a determination to uncover the truth bound them together.

"Hey, everyone," Jake greeted, settling into a chair. "I've got something interesting—or maybe unsettling—to share."

Bridget raised an eyebrow, while Izzy and Emma exchanged curious glances. "What is it?" Emma asked.

"I did some digging online," Jake began, leaning in conspiratorially. "Nathan recently ordered one of those genetic testing kits. You know, the ones where you can find out your family history and relatives."

Izzy furrowed her brow. "Why would Nathan do that? And how does it connect to his murder?"

"That's what I'm trying to figure out," Jake admitted. "It's a bit odd, isn't it? I mean, what would prompt someone to delve into their family tree right before they get killed?"

The coffee shop hummed with speculation as the friends mulled over the potential implications of Nathan's genetic testing.

Jake glanced around cautiously before continuing, "We need to be careful. This opens up a whole new avenue of investigation, and it might put us at odds with whoever murdered Nathan and doesn't want this secret revealed."

The group shared a collective nod, understanding the gravity of their discovery as Emma's mind churned with thoughts.

"I can't shake the feeling that the diary might have more clues," Emma confessed, her fingers tracing the rim of her coffee cup. "I remember a mention of a baby, but it didn't make sense at the time. Now, with Nathan's genetic testing, it feels like there might be a connection."

Bridget's eyes widened. "A baby? That wasn't in context with anything else?"

Emma nodded. "It was almost like a random entry, out of place. I couldn't make sense of it then, but now it's haunting me. It could be connected to the genetic testing, right?"

Izzy chimed in, "If Nathan was trying to reconcile the Lindbergs and the Birches because he found out he was somehow connected to both families, a mention of a baby could be a crucial link. Maybe someone in the past tried to bury a family secret, and now it's resurfacing."

"I'm going to go through the diary more carefully," Emma declared, a determined gleam in her eyes. "If there's any clue hidden in those pages, I'll find it."

The next day, the friends gathered at the edge of Whispering Pines Lake. They sat together on a park bench overlooking the waters of the lake. A loon hooted did in the distance. It was a beautiful picture-perfect Minnesota summer. And yet the cold shoulder that everyone in town was giving them made it feel almost like a Minnesota winter. Together the friends looked through the diary.

After what felt like an eternity, Emma's eyes widened with realization. "Here," she whispered, pointing to an entry that had escaped her notice before. "It talks about a hushed affair. I guess I thought the word affair could mean almost anything. A feud between bakeries, for example. But maybe it means an actual love affair! The names are obscured, but the implications are clear."

Bridget gasped. "A forbidden love? This could be the scandal that tore the families apart. And now, with Nathan's genetic testing, he might have stumbled upon the truth."

Izzy leaned in, her eyes scanning the faded words. "If this secret involves a child born out of a forbidden love, and that child has descendants in both the Lindbergs and the Birches, it would explain why Nathan felt compelled to mend the rift."

Emma closed the diary with a determined look. "We need to find out who that child was, and if they left any traces in the present. It could be the key to understanding Nathan's murder. Jake, you said Nathan ordered some genetic testing. Were you able to find the results?"

"No," Jake said. "I only found evidence that he had ordered one. I'm not sure if they would email him the results or send a hardcopy in the mail. But I'll do a little digging."

Emma gave a small smile. "I will see if Detective Lindberg can find anything."

Bridget gave her an interesting smile. "Emma! Is there something you want to tell us about you and Detective Lindberg?"

Emma smiled back. "No, there's nothing I would like to tell you."

Her friends all laughed. "Fine be that way," Izzy said, "just keep your information to yourself. None of us will have any suspicions."

Emma felt her cheeks flush. "There's nothing to say. I just think he might be willing to help."

Chapter 7

The morning sun painted soft hues across Emma's cozy apartment as her high school friend Lucy, Lucille's granddaughter, knocked on the door. Emma opened it, greeted by the somber expression on Lucy's face.

"Hey, Lucy. Come on in," Emma invited, concern etching her features. Lucy stepped inside, her eyes reflecting a mix of sorrow and confusion.

"I... I needed to talk, Emma," Lucy began, her voice wavering. "I can't believe Nathan's gone. It's tearing me apart."

Emma guided Lucy to the comfortable living room area, offering her a seat on the plush sofa. "I can't believe it either. We're all still trying to make sense of it. How are you holding up?"

Lucy sighed, running a hand through her hair. "It's tough. I mean, he was my cousin, you know? We grew up together. It's hard to fathom that he's just gone."

They sat in a contemplative silence for a moment, the weight of Nathan's absence hanging in the air.

Lucy shifted the conversation, attempting to bring a sliver of normalcy. "I heard about your bakery. It's closed, right? It's a shame."

Emma nodded, a pained expression crossing her face. "Yeah, the police think there might be some connection between Nathan's murder and my bakery. They're treating it as a crime scene."

Lucy's eyes widened with realization. "Oh, wow. That's rough. What do you think about it?"

Emma sighed, her brows furrowing. "I don't know. I just want them to find the real killer and clear my name. The town's changed a lot since all this happened."

Lucy bit her lip, contemplating how much to share. "Speaking of bakeries, Grandma's bakery is getting a lot more business now. With yours closed and all."

Emma gave a small smile. "I'm glad something good is coming of all this. How is your grandma doing?"

"She's not doing too well. I think she's very shaken up by Nathan's murder. As we all are. She's having some struggles with her memory. And she keeps talking about the good old days when she owned your bakery. I think she misses the cozy atmosphere. Her new bakery is great, but it's just not like the old one. You've done a great job of keeping up the spirit of the old bakery. The whole town appreciates that."

Emma's eyes widened in surprise. "Wait, your grandma owned my bakery before me?"

Lucy nodded, her expression apologetic. "Yeah, several years ago. She had to sell it because of some financial issues." Lucy hesitated, her gaze dropping. "Not exactly. Grandma's struggling with early onset dementia. It's been tough on all of us."

Emma's eyes grew sad. "Dementia? Jim had mentioned that. I'm so sorry, Lucy."

"It's okay. We're doing our best to take care of her," Lucy reassured, her eyes reflecting a mixture of sadness and resilience.

The conversation shifted towards Lucille's bakery, now more bustling due to Emma's temporary closure. Lucy continued, "It's just been really hard. Grandma's not the same, you know? She used to run the bakery, and now it's like... like she's losing pieces of herself. She has these angry outbursts. I didn't even know she knew swear words!"

Both women gave each other a small smile. It was almost funny, but also not funny.

Emma couldn't help but empathize with Lucy's plight. "That's heartbreaking. If there's anything I can do to help, please let me know."

"Thanks for letting me talk, Emma. It means a lot," Lucy said, a mix of gratitude and sorrow in her eyes.

Emma offered a sympathetic smile. "Anytime, Lucy. We're all in this together."

A knock echoed through the apartment. Opening the door, she found Detective Lindberg standing there, a composed expression on his face. "Good morning, Emma. Mind if I come in for a moment?"

"Of course, Detective," Emma replied, stepping aside to let him in.

Detective Lindberg still just inside the door in the entryway. "I wanted to check in and see how you're holding up. I can only imagine how difficult this is for you." He was standing in just a little closer, then, was absolutely necessary, and Emma felt her cheeks flush again.

"It's been tough, Detective."

"I wanted to let you know that your bakery is no longer a crime scene. You can return to it now."

Emma's eyes widened, a mixture of surprise and gratitude washing over her. "That's great news! Does that mean the investigation is progressing?"

He nodded. "We're making headway, and your cooperation has been invaluable. If you find anything in that diary or come across any new leads, please keep me informed."

"Of course, Detective," Emma replied, a renewed sense of purpose in her voice.

He tipped his head, and his eyes met hers. "Call me Daniel," he said. "We don't need to use formal titles like Detective."

Emma glance over her shoulder, aware of Lucy listening in. "Oh! Very well, Daniel. Um, just so you know, Lucy's here as well. She's taking Nathan's death pretty hard."

Detective Lindberg stepped back looking slightly embarrassed. "Oh! I didn't realize she was here. I'm sorry if I'm interrupting."

"Not at all," Lucy said stepping into the entryway. "I was just leaving. Thank you so much for your help, Emma. I'll see you later."

As the door closed behind Lucy, Detective Lindberg—Daniel, Emma reminded herself—looked a little flustered. "Sorry for barging in like that. I really didn't know anyone else was here. I know you've been through a lot. I wanted to ask if you'd like to join me for dinner tonight. We could go to Luigi's, that little Italian place in town."

Emma felt a subtle mix of surprise and intrigue. "Dinner? Like a date?" she inquired, her cheeks warming with a hint of curiosity.

Daniel's gaze held a touch of sheepishness. "Well, that depends on how you'd like to think about it. We can keep it professional or... not. Up to you."

Caught off guard by the unexpected invitation, Emma hesitated. A playful spark glinted in Detective Lindberg's eyes, leaving her torn between the allure of a more personal connection and the boundaries of professionalism. "Sure, dinner sounds good," she finally agreed, a subtle smile playing on her lips.

The soft glow of the Italian restaurant cast a warm ambiance around Emma and Daniel. They sat at a corner table, surrounded by the quiet hum of conversation and the tantalizing aroma of Italian spices. The evening seemed promising, yet an undercurrent of tension lingered beneath the surface.

As they delved into a discussion about the diary, Emma couldn't shake the feeling of unease. "Detective—I mean, Daniel, there's something in the diary that's bothering me," she began, her eyes fixed on the candle flickering between them. "A mention of a baby. It's out of context, like it's part of a bigger story. I didn't understand it then, but now, I'm wondering if it could be related to Nathan's genetic testing."

Daniel's brows furrowed slightly. "A baby? That's intriguing. Do you think Nathan found something in his genetic testing that links back to the family feud?"

Emma contemplated the possibility, her fingers tracing the rim of her wine glass. "It's hard to say, but the diary hints at something big happening back then. If there's a connection to Nathan's genetic testing, it might have repercussions on the Lindberg-Birch feud."

Their conversation danced between the lines of the investigation, weaving through uncertainties and potential revelations. As their entrees arrived, Emma couldn't ignore the intensity in Daniel's gaze. His eyes lingered on hers, a subtle undercurrent sparking a mix of emotions. She had never noticed how blue they were.

Just as Emma was about to express her concerns, a voice cut through the air from a nearby table. "Detective Lindberg, fancy seeing you here," called out a woman who had been observing them from a distance. She had an air of authority, and her tone held a hint of polite curiosity.

Daniel acknowledged her with a nod. "Jessie, this is Emma Harper, owner of Northern Pines Pastry. Emma, Officer Jessie Lindberg, my sister."

Oh! Emma thought. The police officer who had been investigating Nathan's murder was related to him! Jessie extended a hand, and Emma shook it, for some reason feeling an unexpected sense of disquiet.

Jessie joined them at their table, a subtle shift in the atmosphere accompanying her presence. "So, what brings you two together outside of official police business?" she inquired, a knowing smile playing on her lips.

Daniel hesitated, glancing briefly at Emma before explaining, "We were discussing the diary Emma found. There's a mention of a baby, and we were exploring if it might be connected to Nathan's genetic testing."

Jessie's expression shifted, a hint of discomfort surfacing. "A baby? That's an unexpected twist. What family are we talking about?"

Emma looked between the two. She suddenly realized that Daniel was, by family connection, related to the feud in town. Could he be completely objective? What was his sister's implication and asking which family they were talking about?

Was she concerned about her own family's reputation? Feeling uncertain, she tried to change the subject.

"I'm sure it's nothing. Just an old diary. I'm sure it has nothing to do with this investigation." She took a sip of wine, wishing that Daniel's sister would leave.

Daniel's features tightened, a subtle defensive note entering his voice. "Actually, I believe Emma's insights from the diary might hold crucial information."

Jessie's scrutiny lingered, and Emma sensed a growing tension between the siblings. They tried to make small talk, but everything felt awkward. Jessie excused herself abruptly before dessert, leaving Daniel and Emma to navigate the lingering awkwardness.

Daniel offered a slightly apologetic glance. "I'm sorry about that, Emma. Jessie can be... protective."

Emma managed a faint smile, concealing her own unease. "It's okay. I understand family dynamics can be complicated. But is she being protective of your family's reputation? Are you sure that you can be objective in this investigation? Your family is involved, aren't they?"

Daniel's eyes held a sincere intensity as he leaned in slightly. "Emma, I want you to know that my family has nothing to do with Nathan's murder. We're not involved in any way."

Emma met his gaze, a flicker of doubt lingering in her eyes. "How can you possibly know that? You haven't completed your investigation yet. I appreciate your assurance, but if this murder is somehow connected to the old family feud, then your family might be directly involved, whether you're aware of it or not."

Daniel sighed, recognizing the skepticism in Emma's tone. "I'm doing everything I can to solve this case objectively. I wouldn't let any personal ties interfere with my duty."

Yet, Emma's unease persisted. She felt a growing tension within her, torn between trusting him and the lingering suspicions that clung to her like shadows. With a heavy sigh, she pushed her plate away and stood.

"I need some time to process everything," Emma admitted, her gaze reflecting a mix of emotions. "I need some time to think. I'll walk myself home."

Daniel nodded, understanding the weight of uncertainty that hung between them. "Take all the time you need. I'll continue the investigation, and if you find anything in that diary, let me know."

With a small smile, Emma excused herself from the table. The quiet ambiance of the restaurant surrounded her, contrasting with her inner turmoil, as she navigated the cozy space toward the exit. The evening air greeted her as she stepped outside, cool and crisp, mirroring the conflicted thoughts swirling within her.

As Emma through the dimly lit streets of Whispering Pines, the events of the evening replayed in her mind. She found herself sitting on the shores of the lake, pondering the events of the night. The enigma of Daniel's family connection, the weight of the family feud, and the unrelenting need to unravel the mystery of Nathan's murder left her with more questions than answers.

Chapter 8

The comforting scent of cinnamon rolls wafted through Emma's bakery as she busied herself in the kitchen. The decision to bake the sweet treats and take them around town served a dual purpose—reconnecting with the community and gathering information about Nathan's murder. With a basket of warm cinnamon rolls in hand, Emma set out on her quest for answers.

Her first destination was Mrs. Thompson's house, a longtime confidant of the Birch family. The elderly woman welcomed Emma with a kind smile, inviting her into the cozy embrace of her living room. The air was filled with the inviting warmth of baked goods as Emma set the basket on the coffee table.

As they indulged in the freshly baked pastries, Emma subtly shifted the conversation toward the Birch family's history. "Mrs. Thompson, I've been reflecting on the Birch family's past, trying to understand more about what might have led to Nathan's tragic end. Do you have any memories or stories that could shed light on the situation?"

Mrs. Thompson, a repository of the town's history, began to share tales of the Birch family's resilience and the deep bonds they held within the community. Amid seemingly trivial stories, Emma listened intently, hoping to uncover a detail that could unravel the mystery surrounding Nathan's murder.

In the midst of the anecdotes, Mrs. Thompson's narrative took an unexpected turn. She spoke of Lucille's third pregnancy, which had been concealed from the prying eyes of the town until after the baby was born. Emma's curiosity heightened as she processed this revelation. "Hidden pregnancy? Mrs. Thompson, can you tell me more about Lucille's third child?"

The elderly woman sighed, her gaze fixed on a distant memory. "It was a tumultuous time, dear. Lucille managed to keep her pregnancy a secret from the entire town until after the baby was born. There were always questions about that child, whispers and speculation. It was a secret guarded fiercely by the Birch family."

Emma felt a surge of intrigue. The hidden pregnancy added a layer of complexity to the town's history, and she pressed Mrs. Thompson for more details. The elderly woman shared snippets of conversations, the hushed tones that accompanied the mysterious birth, and the questions that lingered in the aftermath.

As Emma left Mrs. Thompson's home, the empty basket now held not just remnants of cinnamon rolls but a crucial piece of information that could lead her closer to the truth.

The late afternoon sun cast a warm glow over the shores of Whispering Pines Lake as Emma gathered with her friends—Izzy, Jake, and Bridget. A blanket was spread on the grass, and the soothing sounds of lapping water provided a backdrop to their conversation.

Izzy, the town's librarian and unofficial historian, shared a knowing look with Emma. "Lucille's hidden pregnancy, Emma, it was Nathan's father. His name was Frank. He passed away a few years ago."

Emma's eyes widened, absorbing the weight of this revelation. The connection between Lucille's secret and Nathan's lineage added another layer of complexity to the already intricate web of Whispering Pines' history.

Jake interjected, his analytical mind already at work. "I'll try even harder to get hold of Nathan's DNA testing results. Maybe it'll shed light on why he was so invested in the Lindberg-Birch history and why someone might have wanted him dead."

As they discussed their findings, the setting sun painted the sky in hues of orange and pink, casting long shadows over the friends deep in conversation.

Emma sighed, gazing out over the serene lake. "It's starting to look like Nathan was trying to mend old wounds, and someone didn't want that to happen."

The friends exchanged glances, a collective determination sparking in their eyes. They had unwittingly become entangled in the threads of a generational feud, the echoes of which reverberated through their lives.

Jake, his mind buzzing with the possibilities of what the DNA testing might reveal, excused himself. "I'll get on this right away. If there's something crucial in Nathan's genetic makeup, it could be the key to unlocking the mystery." He stood up, pulled out his phone and walked a little further along the lakeshore for a private conversation. Emma watched him go wondering who he was calling.

Izzy leaned forward, her eyes reflecting the fading sunlight. "With Lucille going senile and Nathan gone, the Birch family has practically vanished from Whispering Pines. Frank's siblings moved to the Twin Cities after he passed away, leaving only Lucille and Nathan here."

Emma furrowed her brow, contemplating the significance of this detail. "So, if Nathan was indeed trying to reconcile the families and mend the old feud, it was a lonely pursuit. The rest of the Birch family had already moved away."

As they sat in quiet contemplation, Jake rejoined the group, his smartphone in hand. "I managed to contact the company that conducted Nathan's DNA testing. They're willing to share the results with us, given the circumstances."

The friends exchanged glances, the gravity of their quest intensifying. Emma nodded, a determination settling in her eyes. "Let's get to the bottom of this. If there's something in those results that ties Nathan's murder to the Lindberg-Birch history, we need to know."

With that, the group gathered their belongings. The sun had dipped below the horizon, casting a twilight glow over Whispering Pines. The friends set a good night as they walked away from the lakeshore, determined to unravel the mysteries that intertwined the town's history with its present.

Chapter 9

The scent of freshly baked cinnamon rolls wafted through the bakery as Emma arranged the pastries in the display. The rhythmic chime of the doorbell announced a visitor, and when Emma looked up, she found Daniel Lindberg standing at the entrance.

"Hey, Emma," Daniel greeted, a smile on his face. "Mind if I join you for a moment?"

"Of course not. Have a seat," Emma replied, gesturing to the stool across the counter.

Daniel settled in, his expression hopeful. "I was thinking, maybe we could take a walk around the lake later. Clear our heads, you know?"

Emma's eyes lit up with enthusiasm. "That sounds wonderful. I'd love to."

As they shared cinnamon rolls, Emma recounted her conversation with Mrs. Thompson. As the details unfolded, a deep furrow formed on Daniel's forehead, and a shadow of concern crossed his eyes.

"I really think you should stop digging into this. Leave the past in the past," Daniel urged, his tone cautious.

Emma frowned, a mixture of confusion and frustration etching her features. "Why? Are you worried your family might be involved?"

Daniel sighed, running a hand through his hair. "No, I've told you. My family has nothing to do with this. But prying into old wounds won't help anyone. It might just make things worse."

Her eyes narrowed, and a spark of defiance ignited in Emma's gaze. "Why are you so defensive? What are you afraid of?"

"I'm not afraid of anything, and this isn't about my family. It's about you and the safety of this town. Stirring up old rivalries won't solve anything," Daniel insisted, a note of urgency in his voice. Then he sighed. "There's something you should know. My sister, Jessie, she's the lead investigator on Nathan's case. She's been under immense stress, and I worry about how she might react if you keep delving into this. Your actions might complicate things for her."

"Complicate things? I just want to find the truth. How can that be a problem?" Emma asked, frustration bubbling up again.

"Jessie is dedicated to her job, and she seems particularly upset about this case. It's a delicate situation," Daniel explained, his gaze sincere.

Emma felt a mixture of understanding and irritation. "So, what? I'm supposed to stop seeking the truth because it might stress out your sister? That doesn't seem fair."

"I'm not asking you to stop, Emma. I just want you to consider the consequences of your actions," Daniel replied, a note of pleading in his voice. "Nathan was a personal friend to lots of us. This is a delicate case."

"Well," Emma retorted, "I need to know the truth, especially since my bakery was implicated, and I won't stop until I find it."

Daniel finished his cinnamon roll in silence, his expression tight. Finally, he pushed the plate away and stood up. "Maybe the walk around the lake isn't a good idea. If you're going to question my methods, maybe it's best if we don't see each other."

With that, Daniel left the bakery once again, leaving Emma to wrestle with the intricate web of secrets, suspicions, and the weight of her own determination to uncover the truth.

As the golden rays of the evening sun bathed the town of Whispering Pines, Jake entered Emma's bakery with a concerned expression on his face. He approached the counter where Emma was organizing pastries.

"Hey, Emma, can we talk for a moment? I've got something important to share with you," Jake said, his tone serious.

Intrigued and slightly worried by the urgency in Jake's voice, Emma set down the cinnamon rolls she was holding. "Sure, Jake. What's going on?"

Jake motioned toward the back of the bakery, away from prying ears. "Let's step into the kitchen. I don't want anyone overhearing this."

In the quiet solitude of the bakery's kitchen, Jake took a deep breath before revealing what was weighing on his mind. "I managed to get Nathan's DNA testing results. There's something...unexpected."

Emma's eyes widened. "What did you find?"

Jake hesitated before speaking, choosing his words carefully. "It turns out that Nathan had significant Lindberg family genes. And that's odd, considering he's a Birch, and the two families hated each other. I didn't want to discuss this here. Meet me, Izzy, and Bridget at the lake shore after work. We need to talk."

Emma nodded, her mind racing with questions. "I'll be there."

The rest of the day passed in a blur for Emma. Her thoughts were consumed by the mysterious revelation Jake had shared. As she closed up the bakery, the anticipation of the impending discussion at the lake weighed on her.

The familiar shores of Whispering Pines Lake greeted Emma as she arrived, finding Jake, Izzy, and Bridget already gathered near the water's edge, swatting mosquitoes.

"Emma, you made it!" Jake exclaimed, his expression a mix of concern and determination.

Emma joined the group. "Okay, Jake, tell us everything. What did you find in Nathan's DNA testing?"

Jake took a deep breath. "Nathan had direct Lindberg family ancestry. In fact, he is first cousins with Detective Lindberg and his sister, Officer Lindberg."

The group fell silent, the lapping waters of the lake serving as a backdrop to their contemplation.

Finally, Emma spoke. "Well, this is certainly interesting. Wait until I tell you about my conversation with Detective Lindberg earlier today. Daniel—I mean, Detective Lindberg came by the bakery today," Emma began.

Izzy raised an eyebrow. "Daniel?"

Emma rolled her eyes. "It wasn't like that. But he asked me to keep quiet about the things I've found in the diary. He said his sister, Jessie, is stressed about the investigation."

Bridget leaned forward, curiosity etched on her face. "Why would Jessie be stressed? And why does Detective Lindberg care so much about what you're doing?"

"That's what I'm trying to figure out," Emma replied, her brow furrowed. "Jessie is his sister, and Daniel seemed genuinely concerned."

Jake chimed in, "Did he say anything else? Anything about why Jessie is stressed or what she might know?"

Emma nodded. "He didn't give me specifics. But he made it clear that I should stay out of the investigation. I can't help but wonder if there's more to the story, especially since Jessie and Daniel are first cousins with Nathan. She couldn't have murdered Nathan, could she? Could she have a motive? And why is Daniel trying to stop me?"

Bridget added, "Daniel's involvement might not be as simple as him just being a detective. He's a Lindberg, too. Maybe he's protecting his family's secrets."

The group fell into a contemplative silence, each contemplating the intricate web of connections that seemed to entangle everyone in Whispering Pines. The moon rose over the lake, lending an ethereal atmosphere to their discussion.

Finally, Emma broke the silence. "We need to be careful. I can't shake the feeling that there's more to discover. Whatever secrets this town holds, we're on the brink of uncovering them. And if Officer Lindberg is a murderer, then we have a serious problem with the police department. I don't know who we can turn to."

As they left the lake shore, the mystery of Whispering Pines deepened, leaving Emma and her friends with more questions than answers.

Chapter 10

Emma, determined to unravel the mysteries that seemed to intertwine with the history of Whispering Pines, decided to pay Lucille a visit. Armed with a small basket containing chamomile tea, an old tea set, and delicate teacups, Emma hoped to connect with Lucille through the fond memories of her youth.

Lucille had been known for hosting elegant tea parties during her younger years, a detail Emma remembered from the tales circulating in the close-knit community. Perhaps, through the comforting ritual of a tea party, Emma could coax Lucille into sharing insights that lingered in the recesses of her memory.

The summer day was quiet as Emma approached Lucille's house. The porch creaked under her weight as she carefully navigated the steps. She could see the lace curtains gently swaying through the windows, hinting at the tranquil atmosphere inside.

Taking a deep breath, Emma knocked on Lucille's door, her heart fluttering with a mix of anticipation and apprehension. The door opened slowly, revealing Lucille standing in the dimly lit foyer.

"Hello, Lucille," Emma greeted with a warm smile. "I brought some things for a tea party. Do you mind if I come in?"

Lucille regarded her with a mix of curiosity and uncertainty but gestured for Emma to enter. The air inside was musty, carrying the weight of years gone by. As Emma set up the tea party in Lucille's quaint living room, memories of the past seemed to echo in the quiet corners of the house.

"I thought we could have a tea party, just like the ones you used to host," Emma explained, pouring fragrant chamomile tea into the delicate cups. "Sometimes, the familiar rituals help us remember beautiful moments."

Lucille's eyes flickered with a glimmer of recognition as she observed the tea set. Emma handed her a cup, the porcelain cool against her weathered hands.

"Lucille, do you remember the lovely tea parties you used to organize?" Emma asked gently, her tone laced with nostalgia.

Lucille stared into the cup, the steam rising and carrying with it the essence of chamomile. A smile played on her lips, and she nodded faintly.

As Emma engaged Lucille in conversation, the room gradually filled with the soft hum of shared memories. Lucille seemed to come back to herself. She reminisced about the laughter, the clinking of teacups, and the warmth of companionship with the other young mothers, in whispering Pines back in the days when she was young mother, herself.

Finally, as the tea party unfolded in a dance of recollections, Emma seized the opportunity to gently broach the subject that had been haunting her thoughts—the Birch family, the Lindbergs, and the enigmatic details embedded in Lucille's past.

"Lucille, there's something I wanted to ask you about. Do you remember your son, Frank?"

Lucille's gaze flickered, and a cloud seemed to pass over her eyes. "Frank passed away. I miss him."

"I'm so sorry," Emma said. "That must be extremely painful."

A single tear rolled down Lucille's cheek and fell into her teacup. "My mother said I must never let anyone find out."

Emma stared at her. "That Frank died? But the whole town was at his funeral. You must never let anyone find out what?"

Lucille shook her head. "I must never let anyone find out. No matter what. That's what mother said. And I am an obedient daughter. I would never bring shame to my parents." She took another sip of her tea, her hands trembling. Her eyes had a bacon expression now, and Emma realized the old woman was no longer mentally present.

As Emma cleared away the remnants of their tea party, carefully placing the delicate teacups back into the basket, her eyes wandered to Lucille's kitchen counter. Amongst the familiar ingredients for baking, something caught Emma's attention—a box of rat poison, inconspicuously placed next to the flour and sugar.

A frown creased Emma's forehead as she regarded the peculiar addition. Why would rat poison be in Lucille's kitchen? She hesitated, contemplating whether to bring it up, but the need for clarity overwhelmed her.

"L-Lucille, what's this?" Emma pointed to the box of rat poison, her voice gentle yet laced with concern.

Lucille followed Emma's gaze, her eyes resting on the foreign object. However, instead of recognition, her expression remained blank, devoid of any understanding.

"Rat poison?" Lucille echoed, her brows furrowing as she examined the item. "I don't remember buying any rat poison. Are you sure it's mine?"

Emma hesitated, a disquieting feeling settling in the pit of her stomach. Lucille's lack of recognition was unsettling. Could it be a simple mistake, or was there something more sinister lurking beneath the surface?

"I... I thought maybe you might have used it for something," Emma replied, her words cautious. "But if you don't remember, it's probably nothing. Maybe it got mixed up with the baking supplies."

Emma finished clearing away the remnants of their tea party, all the while unable to shake the unsettling image of the rat poison from her mind. As she left Lucille's house, the air outside felt as thick with unanswered questions as it was with mosquitoes.

That night, as Emma lay in bed, the weight of uncertainty pressed upon her. The connection between Lucille, the rat poison, and the unfolding mysteries of the town gnawed at her consciousness.

The following morning, Emma couldn't shake the need for answers. Determination etched on her face, she resolved to delve deeper into the enigma that surrounded Lucille's kitchen. Emma opened the door to her bakery, the familiar scent of pastries and cinnamon rolls doing little to ease the turmoil within.

Lucille's bakery was just three blocks over from Emma's. Emma crossed the threshold, the chime above the door announcing her arrival. Lucille stood behind the counter, arranging pastries with a distant expression.

"Lucille, about the rat poison..." Emma began tentatively, the weight of her words hanging in the air.

Lucille looked up, her eyes meeting Emma's with a hint of confusion. "Rat poison? What are you talking about, dear?"

Emma's heart sank, realization dawning. Lucille's response was not an act; she genuinely had no recollection of the box of rat poison in her kitchen.

Back in her own bakery, Emma stood still, staring at the ingredients for homemade bread, the revelation from her visit with Lucille echoing in her mind like a recipe finally falling into place, forming a chilling picture. Nathan, the gentle peacemaker, poisoned with rat poison from Lucille's kitchen? The connection sent shivers down Emma's spine. The question lingered, heavy in the air: was Lucille the murderer, or was someone else pulling the strings?

And if she couldn't go to the police, who should she tell? Emma's phone rang. Dusting off her hands, she pulled out her phone and answered a call from Izzy.

Chapter 11

"Emma, you won't believe what I found in the Towne archives. Meet us on the shores of the lake; it's something we can't discuss over the phone," Izzy exclaimed.

Intrigued and slightly anxious, Emma agreed, her mind already racing with the possibilities of what Izzy might have uncovered. Gathering her belongings, she locked the bakery, the familiar creak of the door now carrying a weight of anticipation.

At the lake, the soft ripples of water provided a gentle soundtrack to their meeting. Emma's friends, Izzy, Bridget, and Jake, waited by the water's edge, their expressions a blend of excitement and concern. The fading sunlight painted the scene with hues of orange and pink, casting a tranquil veil over the significant discussion that awaited them.

"What did you find?" Emma asked, her curiosity bubbling beneath the surface.

Izzy took a deep breath. "I delved into the Towne archives, searching for any historical ties between the Lindbergs and Birches. And I found something, Emma. Something that might unravel the mysteries surrounding Nathan's murder."

"I found Frank Birch's birth certificate. Lucille is listed as the mother, but the father is marked as John Doe."

A murmur of surprise and understanding rippled through the group. Bridget, ever pragmatic, commented,

"Illegitimate births weren't uncommon back then. What's the big deal?"

Izzy, her eyes carrying the gravity of her revelation, responded, "It's not just that. I found another document. It suggests that the real father was Barney Lindberg."

A stunned silence settled over the group. The implications of Izzy's words echoed against the backdrop of the lake, the tranquility of the evening disrupted by the revelation.

Emma's mind whirred with realization. The fragments of Lucille's cryptic warnings now fell into place. Her mother's insistence that the truth must remain hidden took on a new, profound meaning. Lucille wasn't safeguarding just any secret; she was shielding the truth about the father of her child. This would've been a scandal of huge proportions in the early 1900s.

"You mean," Emma hesitated, grappling with the enormity of the revelation, "Barney Lindberg was Nathan's grandfather?"

Izzy nodded solemnly. "It seems that way. This discovery could be the spark that ignited the feud between the Lindbergs and Birches."

The group, enveloped in a profound silence, contemplated the implications of this long-buried truth. The lake, a silent witness to the unfolding drama, mirrored the reflections of the past.

Bridget, breaking the stillness, voiced what they were all thinking. "But why keep it a secret? Illegitimate births, family scandals—they're not unheard of. What turned it into a feud?"

Izzy flipped through the papers, revealing more details about the clandestine affair that had sown the seeds of discord. "It wasn't just about a forbidden love affair. It seems that even before Frank's birth, Lucille's family was vehemently against any connection with the Lindbergs. The Lindbergs were the town outcasts. It seems Barney's father had committed some sort of crime, and had a bit of a drinking problem, and nobody wanted their family associated with theirs. So the fact that Lucille had a baby with Barney was shocking to her parents, and would have

52

been shocking to the whole town. I think her family would have felt tainted by the connection to the Lindbergs, as well as by an illegitimate pregnancy. The tensions escalated, leading to the birth certificate concealing the truth. It looks like Lucille married George Birch a few months before the baby was born."

As the pieces of the puzzle fell into place, Emma's shock transformed into a somber acknowledgment of the complexities that had shaped Whispering Pines. The feud between the Lindbergs and Birches, far from a mere clash of personalities, was rooted in a clandestine affair and the societal norms that sought to bury it.

Jake, who had been silently absorbing the unfolding revelation, finally spoke, his voice tinged with a mix of realization and concern. "Guys, this aligns with what I found in Nathan's DNA testing. It showed connections to both the Birch and Lindberg families. He must've discovered the truth about his heritage, about Barney Lindberg being his grandfather."

Emma's mind churned with the implications. Nathan, in his quest to uncover his roots, had stumbled upon a legacy of betrayal and clandestine affairs. The DNA testing, meant to illuminate his ancestry, had illuminated the dormant embers of a long-buried feud.

Bridget, pragmatic as ever, broke the contemplative silence. "So, what does this mean for Nathan's murder? How does the knowledge of his true lineage tie into his death?"

Izzy, her eyes focused on the distant horizon, offered a speculative hypothesis. "Perhaps someone in the family couldn't bear the revelation. The truth surfacing might have reignited old wounds, threatening to expose a history of deception."

Emma took a deep breath, her words measured as she shared her recent conversation with Lucille. "When I visited Lucille earlier, I noticed a box of rat poison in her kitchen. When I asked her about it, she seemed confused, as if she didn't even know it was there. But what struck me was what she said about her mother. She mentioned her mother warning her never to let anyone find out something. Given what Izzy just shared about Barney Lindberg potentially being Nathan's grandfather, Lucille's secret was likely the father of her child."

Izzy's eyes widened in realization. "Lucille's mother was probably referring to the affair between Barney Lindberg and Lucille, resulting in Nathan's father, Frank Birch. If Nathan discovered this truth through the DNA testing, it could explain why Lucille is so distressed."

Bridget interjected with a touch of skepticism, "But why would Lucille poison her own grandson? If anything, she'd want to protect him."

Emma nodded, acknowledging the complexity. "I don't think Lucille would intentionally harm Nathan. Lucille's mind is clouded by dementia. I noticed signs of it when I was at her place. She may not fully understand what she's doing. It's like she's stuck in a loop, obeying her mother's command from decades ago. The fear instilled in her back then, combined with the confusion of her present state, might have led her to believe that she needed to silence Nathan."

Izzy furrowed her brow, contemplating the tragic twist of fate. "So, Lucille might have seen Nathan's discovery as a threat not just to herself but to her family's carefully guarded secret. And in her distorted reality, silencing Nathan was a way to protect that secret."

Bridget sighed, the weight of the revelation settling in. "It's heartbreaking to think that Lucille, who's been a part of this town for so long, could do such a thing."

Jake nodded in agreement. "Exactly. But it all makes sense. At least, in a 'dementia' sort of way. How terribly tragic. What do we do now?"

But Emma's thoughts were on another aspect of the investigation. "So, Daniel wasn't covering up his family's involvement. But his protective stance toward his sister is still puzzling. Why would Jessie be stressed about this investigation unless there's more to the story?"

Emma sighed, looking out over the rippling waters of the lake. "I need to talk to Daniel. Maybe he knows more about the family dynamics or if there's someone else involved. If Jessie isn't the mastermind behind this, then who is? And why was she so concerned about Nathan's murder?"

Bridget, usually a beacon of optimism, now wrestled with worries etched across her face. "If we go to Detective Lindberg, what will happen to Lucille?" she questioned, her voice laden with concern. "Is she really guilty if she has dementia? Can someone with her condition be held responsible for murder?"

The trio exchanged glances, grappling with the complexity of their discovery. Izzy chimed in, "We can't determine legal implications, but we have a moral duty to bring this to the authorities. Lucille may not fully comprehend her actions, but if there's a chance she committed a crime, it needs to be investigated."

Emma nodded, the weight of responsibility settling upon her shoulders. "We can't let our emotions cloud our judgment. We're not here to pass judgment; we're here to uncover the truth."

Bridget said, "But what if Detective Lindberg doesn't believe us? What if he thinks we're just concocting stories?"

Jake chimed in, "We've got evidence – the birth certificate, the DNA testing, Lucille's confusion – it all points to a deeper truth. We have to trust the system to sift through the facts. It's not our role to decide guilt or innocence."

The moon cast a pale glow on the lake's surface, illuminating the scene as the friends huddled by the shore. In the distance, the rhythmic croaking of frogs echoed through the tranquil night. As they exchanged final thoughts on their decision to approach Detective Lindberg, a sudden intrusion disrupted their contemplation.

Approaching from the shadows, Officer Blankenship and Officer Jessie Lindberg emerged, their figures silhouetted against the moonlit water. The creaking of the wooden dock beneath his boots was the harbinger of an unsettling revelation. Emma looked up, her eyes meeting the stern gaze of the law.

"Emma Harper," Officer Blankenship's voice cut through the quiet night like a chilling breeze. "You're under arrest."

Confusion flickered across Emma's face, her friends sharing a collective gasp. "Under arrest? For what?" Emma questioned, her voice tinged with disbelief.

Officer Blankenship's stoic expression offered no reprieve. "You're being charged with the murder of Nathan Birch."

Chapter 12

Shock reverberated through the group, their unity unraveling in the face of an unexpected accusation. Emma's friends exchanged glances, a mixture of disbelief and concern etched on their faces. Bridget stammered, "But she didn't—"

The officer interrupted, "We have evidence linking you to the crime. You'll have a chance to defend yourself in court. You have the right to remain silent. Anything you say can be used against you in a court of law. Do you understand?"

Emma gaped at him. "No. I don't understand at all. You have the wrong person. I had nothing to do with this."

Jessie Lindberg spoke up. "You have been in all of the places where anything suspicious is connected to this crime. And your pastries were the last ones that Nathan ate before he died. Save the sob story Emma. You can tell us about it in court."

As Officer Blankenship handcuffed Emma, her friends all began speaking at once.

Officer Blankenship interrupted them. "You might want to be quiet, or the things that you say might be used against Emma in court as well."

They fell silent and watched in horror is Emma was walked toward a police car and ushered into the backseat.

Emily and her head against the seat of the squad car, wondering how things could possibly have come to this.

The police station loomed in the dim glow of streetlights, casting long shadows on the quiet town. Emma was ushered inside by Officer Blankenship, her mind grappling with the surreal progression of events. The muted sounds of the small station echoed through the sterile walls.

As they reached the booking area, Jessie Lindberg stood with a stern expression, her gaze fixed on Emma. Officer Blankenship began the routine process of booking, reading Emma her rights again and collecting personal information. Jessie's presence heightened the tension, each glance from her an unspoken accusation.

In the midst of the procedural formalities, Daniel entered the room, his eyes meeting Emma's briefly before focusing on the paperwork in front of him. Emma took a deep breath, gathering her resolve.

"Detective Lindberg," Emma addressed him, her voice steady despite the anxiety that churned within. "Can I talk to you about Nathan's murder?"

Detective Lindberg raised an eyebrow, glancing at Officer Blankenship. "Would you like an attorney present?" he asked, a note of caution in his voice.

Emma hesitated, considering the weight of her words. "No, I just want to tell you what I know. It might help."

The detective regarded her for a moment before nodding. "Fine. Let's step into my office."

As they entered the detective's office, the door closed behind them, muffling the distant hum of the station. Emma took a seat, her hands trembling slightly. Detective Lindberg sat across from her, waiting for her to begin.

With a deep breath, Emma recounted the unraveling tale—the hidden affair, Lucille's secret, and the strained ties between the Lindbergs and the Birches. The detective listened intently, his expression revealing little.

"So, Lucille Birch might have killed Nathan because he found out about the family secret, his grandfather's birth father," Emma concluded, her eyes searching Daniel's face for a reaction.

The detective leaned back in his chair, contemplating the revelation. "If what you're saying is true, it adds a new layer to the case. But we need evidence. Lucille having a motive isn't enough."

Emma nodded, understanding the gravity of the situation. "I think we have the evidence. You should talk to Jake and Izzy."

Detective Lindberg regarded her with a measured gaze. "I appreciate your cooperation, Emma. We'll look into it. In the meantime, you'll have to stay in the holding cell until we sort things out."

As Emma was led back to the holding area, uncertainty lingered in the air. The door closed behind her, leaving her alone with the weight of her revelations and the anticipation of what the investigation would unveil. The wheels of justice were set in motion, each turn revealing the intricate threads of a seemingly innocent town's dark tapestry.

Inside the confines of the holding cell, Emma's nerves churned with restless anticipation. The sterile walls seemed to close in on her, and the silence of the police station pressed against her eardrums. Through the dim light filtering into the cell, she strained to catch glimpses of the activity beyond.

Voices murmured in the distance, and the occasional shuffle of footsteps echoed through the corridor. Emma leaned against the cold metal bars, watching the entrance as if expecting a revelation with each passing moment. The suspense weighed heavily on her.

Suddenly, the station door swung open, and Officer Blankenship approached Emma's cell with a stoic expression. "Your friends are here," he announced.

A mixture of relief and curiosity surged within Emma. "What's going on? Can you tell me?"

Officer Blankenship shook his head. "Sorry, but I can't provide details. You'll have to wait."

As the officer led Emma to a small room designated for meetings, she saw Jake, Izzy, and Bridget seated across from Daniel and his sister, Jessie. The atmosphere in the room was tense, a palpable energy that Emma couldn't quite decipher.

The friends exchanged fleeting glances as Emma took her seat, questions lingering in her eyes. Detective Lindberg, looking as impassive as ever, finally spoke. "Your friends here have been assisting with the investigation. We're trying to piece everything together."

Emma's heart pounded in her chest. But Jessie's gaze hardened, and Detective Lindberg interjected, "We're still assessing the situation. Now, your friends mentioned that Lucille might have some valuable information."

Bridget nodded, her eyes reflecting concern. "We told them about Lucille's confusion and the secret she's been keeping for years. But we think that you need to tell him about your conversation with her. About her confusion about her mother."

Emma told Daniel and his sister and Officer Blankenship who had come in to listen all about her conversation with Lucille. And about seeing the rat poison in the kitchen next to the baking supplies.

Detective Lindberg leaned back, studying Emma intently. "We're looking into it, but I can't promise anything. Lucille's current state might complicate matters."

Emma glanced at Jake, Izzy, and Bridget, silently conveying her gratitude for their support. The investigation had taken an unforeseen turn, and the consequences remained unclear.

As the meeting concluded, Officer Blankenship escorted Emma back to the holding cell. Alone once more, she sank onto the narrow bench wondering what would happen next.

Chapter 13

The cold, unforgiving metal bench in the holding cell offered little comfort as Emma anxiously awaited answers. The muffled sounds of the police station seeped through the cracks in the walls, and her ears perked up as she recognized the approach of Officer Blankenship and another set of hesitant footsteps.

A subdued shuffle of uncertain footsteps, accompanied Officer Blankenship, and Emma's heart quickened with curiosity. As Officer Blankenship led the new arrival into the precinct, Lucille's familiar voice, though slightly shaky, reached Emma's ears.

"I don't understand what's happening," Lucille's voice said, flooding back to Emma from the front of the police station.

"Lucille Birch, you are being brought in for questioning in connection to the murder of Nathan Birch. You have the right to remain silent..."

The Miranda rights echoed through the confined space, and Emma's eyes widened in disbelief. As Lucille stepped around the corner, Emma could see her. Lucille, wrapped in an old shawl, appeared fragile against the stern backdrop of law enforcement. A swirl of conflicting emotions engulfed Emma — concern for Lucille and a renewed sense of urgency to understand the unfolding situation.

Lucille's soft-spoken words trickled into the air as she responded to the standard protocol. Emma strained to catch the essence of their exchange, her mind grappling with the implications. The arrest of an elderly woman, seemingly frail and caught in the web of her own memories, felt surreal against the backdrop of the dimly lit cell.

Detective Lindberg's footsteps echoed down the sterile corridor. "Lucille, I'd like you to meet Dr. Elizabeth Stevens. She's here to help us understand your perspective and ensure everything is done fairly," Detective Lindberg's voice, reassuring and measured, cut through the ambient noise.

The gentle cadence of Dr. Stevens' voice followed, a soothing counterpoint to the stark atmosphere of the precinct. Emma strained to hear her words. "Hello, Lucille. I'm Dr. Stevens, and I'm here to talk with you. We'll take our time and go at your pace, okay?"

Lucille's soft response, laden with a mix of confusion and compliance, filtered through the cell's barriers. Emma, still confined, found solace in the idea that Lucille was not alone in this disorienting moment.

Lucille was taken into a back room, and everything was quiet for quite a while. Emma sat back in her cell and wondered what was happening.

After what felt like forever, Detective Lindberg approached the holding cell.

"Emma, all charges against you have been dropped. It seems there was a mistake," he said, a mix of apology and concern in his voice.

Relief flooded Emma, and a knot of tension she hadn't realized was there began to loosen. "A mistake? I should certainly say so! What happened?"

Detective Lindberg sighed, his gaze momentarily dropping before meeting hers again. "It's a complicated situation. I'll explain everything, but first, are you okay?"

Emma hesitated, absorbing the weight of the night's events. "I... I think so," she replied, still uncertain about the tumultuous emotions roiling within her.

The detective's eyes softened, genuine concern evident in his features. "I understand this has been incredibly difficult for you. If you need anything—"

Before he could finish, Emma took a step back, creating a subtle but clear distance. "I appreciate that, Detective, but right now, I'm not sure how I feel about you. You believed I was guilty."

He shook his head. "Emma, I never believed you were guilty. But I can't stop and investigation just because of my own feelings."

Emma studied his face, grappling with conflicting emotions. "Why did you believe your sister over me? I... I need some time, Detective."

"Please Emma, please call me Daniel. Take all the time you need. But it's late, and I would like to walk you home. I want to explain everything about Jessie and the accusations. It's the least I can do."

Emma hesitated, contemplating the offer. The night had taken its toll, leaving her emotionally drained, and the prospect of an explanation seemed like a lifeline amid the chaos. After a moment, she nodded. "Okay, Detective. Walk me home."

He winced at her choice not to use his given name as he unlocked the cell and let her out.

The night air was crisp as Daniel walked alongside Emma, the rhythmic sound of their footsteps echoing in the quiet streets. The moon cast a gentle glow on the path, and the distant murmur of the lake added to the tranquil ambiance.

"I want to apologize again, Emma," Daniel began, his voice carrying a weight of sincerity. "Jessie's emotions got the best of her. I don't know if you're aware, but she was dating Nathan, and when she found out about his death, it hit her hard. She couldn't think straight."

Emma listened, her gaze fixed on the pavement, absorbing his words. The revelation about Jessie and Nathan's relationship added a layer of complexity to the already convoluted situation.

"Seeing Nathan with you at the festival, I think it made her anxious," Daniel continued, his tone genuine. "She believed something happened between you two that might have hurt him.

I tried to reason with her, to tell her that it wasn't your fault, but she was convinced."

Emma's steps slowed as they approached the lake, its surface reflecting the moonlight. She took a deep breath, attempting to process the newfound information. "So, she accused me because she thought I hurt Nathan?"

Daniel nodded, a mixture of regret and frustration evident on his face. "I fought for you, Emma. I argued that you weren't guilty. I know you, and I believe in you. I always have."

They walked along the lakeside path, the cool breeze carrying with it the weight of the night's revelations. Emma appreciated Daniel's candor, but a lingering unease clouded her thoughts.

"I appreciate that, Detective. I do," Emma replied, her voice measured. "But it's not just about Jessie. How could you let them arrest me?"

Daniel sighed, rubbing his temples as he struggled to find the right words. "I was torn between my sister's grief and my trust in you. It was a difficult position to be in. I should have handled it better, and I'm truly sorry. I hope you can understand that it wasn't a lack of trust in you, it was a need to not let my own emotions cloud the investigation. I didn't want to do the same thing. My sister was doing. Letting my emotions get in the way of seeing the investigation clearly. I wasn't certain that I was seeing it clearly because of my feelings for you."

Emma felt her cheeks flush despite the cool night air. They walked in silence for a moment, the waters of the lake lapping gently against the shore. As they reached Emma's house, the glow from the porch light spilled onto the front steps. He had feelings for her? She must've known that, why else would he have asked her out to dinner? But she had been trying to convince herself that it was only about the investigation. Now he was admitting that it was more than that. And she wasn't sure how she felt about it.

"Thank you for walking me home," Emma said, her eyes reflecting a mixture of gratitude and contemplation.

Daniel nodded, a sincerity in his eyes. "You don't deserve any of this. I hope you can find it in yourself to forgive Jessie and me for the mess we've caused."

Emma hesitated, the weight of the night's events pressing upon her. "I need some time, Daniel. To process everything. Good night."

He smiled. "It's good to hear you call me by my name at least. Good night, Emma," he said, and with that, Daniel turned to leave, leaving Emma standing alone on her porch.

Chapter 14

Emma was nestled in a deep, dreamless sleep when the abrupt knocking on her door jolted her awake. The sound echoed through her harried dreams, leaving her momentarily disoriented. She squinted at the clock and then jumped out of bed! Good heavens how did it get to be so late? Her bakery wasn't even open for business yet today. What would her customers think?

The rhythmic pounding continued, insistent and demanding. Who could be knocking so fervently?

Emma descended the stairs, each step a silent acknowledgment of the peculiar morning unfolding around her. The insistent knocking still echoed in her ears, but as she approached the kitchen, the unmistakable scent of pastries baking wafted through the air.

Her steps quickened as she reached the kitchen door. Pushing it open, she was greeted by a bustling scene – Izzy, Bridget, and Jake donned aprons, moving with a synchronized rhythm as they prepared pastries. The ovens hummed with activity, and the familiar surroundings of her bakery stirred a mixture of emotions.

"Izzy, Bridget, Jake – what's happening?" Emma's voice trembled with a blend of confusion and gratitude.

Izzy, with a mischievous grin, turned around, holding a tray of freshly baked cinnamon rolls. "We thought you might be a little tired this morning. So we opened the bakery for you! You had customers waiting."

Tears welled up in Emma's eyes as she absorbed the gesture of friendship. She thanked her friends with a hug is the knocking on her own front door group even louder.

Stepping out of the kitchen, Emma made her way to her personal apartment's front door. To her surprise, Daniel stood there, a mix of eagerness and relief in his expression.

"Daniel, what are you doing here?" she asked.

He shifted uncomfortably, a faint smile playing on his lips. "Can I come in? There's something important I need to tell you."

Emma nodded, guiding him upstairs into her living room. The scent of baking lingered in the air, a comforting backdrop to the unfolding conversation. As they settled into the room, Daniel began to share the news that had prompted his early visit.

"Dr. Stevens worked out a deal with the police, Lucille, and the attorneys," he explained. "Lucille is going to be admitted to a care facility, where she can get the treatment and care that she needs for her dementia. She was clearly not acting with us in mind. There are no charges being brought, and she is just going to get the care that she needs."

Daniel's revelation about Lucille being admitted to a care facility brought a mix of emotions – relief that Lucille wouldn't face charges and sadness for the decline of a woman who had been part of the town's fabric for so long.

"Thank you for letting me know, Daniel," Emma said, her voice tinged with gratitude.

He nodded, his eyes reflecting a sense of responsibility. "Both my sister and I have been advocating for her, making sure she gets the care she needs. This way, she'll be safe and receive proper attention for her condition."

Emma appreciated his effort on Lucille's behalf. "I'm glad she's getting the help she needs. And it's scary that she could murder someone in her condition. What a tragic situation, but I'm so glad that we were able to find out the truth and get her into the care that she needs."

Relieved, Emma looked up with a smile in her eyes. "Would you like hot cinnamon rolls for breakfast by any chance?"

"Now that you mention it, I am hungry. And cinnamon rolls sound amazing! I believe there is a world-class bakery right downstairs." He gave her a quick wink, and she smiled in return.

The aroma of freshly baked pastries enveloped them as they entered the bakery.

Izzy, Bridget, and Jake looked up from their tasks, expressions transitioning from concentration to smiles as Emma and Daniel entered.

"Good news?" Izzy asked, a hopeful glint in her eyes.

Emma beamed, "Lucille is getting the care she needs, and there won't be any charges against her. Daniel made it happen."

Her friends exchanged smiles, their support unwavering.

"Let's celebrate with breakfast," Emma suggested, leading Daniel to a cozy table by the window.

The familiar chatter of the bakery, coupled with the rich aroma of coffee and cinnamon rolls, provided a backdrop for their shared breakfast. As they savored each bite, Emma found herself grateful for the presence of friends who had rallied around her during a tumultuous time.

"I appreciate everything you've done, Daniel," she said, sipping her coffee. "Without your intervention, things might have turned out differently."

He met her gaze, a sincerity in his eyes. "I just wanted to make things right. For Lucille and for you."

The bell above the door jingled, announcing a new arrival, and Jessie walked in. Memories of the Italian restaurant flashed in Emma's mind, but this time, Jessie seemed different – apologetic, with a sincerity that spoke volumes.

Jessie approached the table, her eyes meeting Emma's with a mix of regret and understanding. "Hey Emma, can I join you?"

Emma nodded, although she wasn't sure how she felt about it. "Of course, Jessie."

Jessie began, "I owe you an apology, Emma. My emotions about Nathan clouded my judgment. I should have been more objective and not let personal feelings interfere with the investigation."

Emma appreciated Jessie's honesty. "We all get caught up in our emotions sometimes. It's part of being human."

Jessie sighed, her demeanor softening. "I'm just relieved to know the truth about Lucille and the rat poison. It's a weight off my shoulders."

Emma nodded, acknowledging the complexity of the situation. "Lucille's going to get the care she needs. It's the best outcome for everyone. Would you like a cinnamon roll, Jessie," Emma offered, gesturing to the delectable treats displayed on the table. "And a cup of coffee? We're celebrating today. And I'd like you to join us in the celebrations."

Jessie's face brightened with a small smile. "Thank you, Emma. I appreciate your kindness."

Under the table, Daniels foot brushed against Emma's. She looked up at him, surprised. And he just smiled at her and left his foot where it was, resting against hers.

Izzy, Jake, and Bridget pulled up chairs during a lull in the busy bakery morning, and the sixth of them discussed everything that happened and Nathan's upcoming funeral service.

After a while, Daniel said that she had to get back to work. She asked Emma if she would walk outside with him.

They made their way to the back of the bakery and back through Emma's on front door away from the busy crowds of the town. Daniel pulled Emma into a hug, and she found that she was grateful for his embrace. She laid her head against his chest.

After a moment, Daniel looked at Emma with a warm smile, his eyes reflecting a mix of gratitude and sincerity. "Emma, I can't thank you enough for how you've handled everything. You're strong, and I appreciate your understanding."

Emma smiled in return, the weight of recent events lifting from her shoulders. "Thank you. It seems like we've just started getting to know each other, and yet we've been through a lot together."

He hugged her again, then took a step back, his gaze lingering on eyes and lips. "You know, I was thinking about next weekend. There's a murder mystery play showing at the Lazy River Dinner Theatre, and I'd love for you to come with me. If things get complicated, maybe we can solve the crime together."

Emma's eyes sparkled with amusement. "A murder mystery play? That sounds right up our alley. I'd love to go."

Daniel's face lit up, and a playful smile crossed his lips. "Great! I can't think of anyone I'd rather have as my partner in crime-solving."

As they shared a lighthearted laugh, the atmosphere between them shifted subtly. There was a moment of shared understanding, and then, without any more hesitation, Daniel leaned in and gently pressed his lips to Emma's. The kiss was soft, a sweet culmination of a journey that had brought them closer together.

When they parted, Daniel's expression held a mix of warmth and sincerity. "If it's OK with you, I'd love to come by for breakfast again tomorrow. And I can pay for the cinnamon rolls! I don't want you to think I'm taking advantage of your hospitality and great baking."

Emma pulled him in for another kiss. "Come by for breakfast any time."

He hugged her, and with a wave, Daniel walked down the quiet street, leaving Emma standing on her doorstep with a contented heart. As she closed the door behind her, she couldn't help but feel a sense of optimism for the future – a future that held not only mysteries to solve- albeit hopefully in the form of dinner theater plays- but also the promise of shared adventures and genuine connection.

EPILOGUE

The golden hues of the evening sun bathed Whispering Pines in a warm glow as Emma, Daniel, Jessie, Jake, Bridget, and Izzy gathered after closing at Emma's bakery. The scent of fresh pastries lingered in the air, creating an inviting atmosphere.

They huddled around a table, their conversation a comforting blend of laughter and shared moments.

"So, who do you think will take over Lucille's bakery?" Bridget mused, her eyes gleaming with anticipation.

Jake chuckled, "Maybe we'll get lucky, and it'll be someone with a passion for baking like Emma here."

Emma grinned, appreciating the sentiment. Then she turned to Jessie. "How are you doing? The funeral was three weeks ago. I know you still miss him. Are you doing OK?"

Jessie said, "I'm doing okay, just taking some time off and planning a canoe trip up north to recharge."

Bridget said, "Classes are starting soon, and I'm ready to dive back into school."

As they chatted, the camaraderie among the friends felt stronger than ever. With the evening winding down, they decided to go to the lakeshore. They walked through town toward the lake as the sun dipped low on the horizon. Jessie brought a couple of loaves of day-old bread, and they tossed bread to the ducks, their laughter echoing against the gentle lapping of the water.

As the group walked on ahead, Daniel and Emma found themselves a little behind the others. Hand in hand, they enjoyed the serenity of the moment. Daniel turned to Emma, his eyes filled with sincerity.

"You're the best partner I've ever had, crime-solving or otherwise," he admitted.

A warmth spread through Emma as their lips met in a tender kiss. The sun dipped below the horizon, casting hues of orange and pink across the sky, a perfect backdrop to the beginning of their shared journey.

Whispering Pines held its mysteries, but in the company of friends and the promise of new adventures, Emma knew that each challenge could be met with resilience and joy. Together, they looked toward the future, ready to embrace whatever it might bring.

LOVELETTER

PUBLICATIONS

EST. 2023

Printed in Great Britain
by Amazon

38991426R00047